THE NO-BARK DOG

THE FOLLETT BEGINNING-TO-READ SERIES

THE NO-

ILLUSTRATIONS BY
TOM O'SULLIVAN

BARK DOG

BY STAN WILLIAMSON

FOLLETT PUBLISHING COMPANY   CHICAGO

Library of Congress Catalog Card Number: 62-15671

SBN   695-46340-3   Titan binding   SBN   695-86340-1   Trade binding   *Seventh Printing*

For Kathy Pierson, for Edward D. Pierson IV,
and all their friends

TIMOTHY TROTTER had a new dog.

His name was Top.

Now it was dog-walking time.

Timothy Trotter put on his hat and his jacket.

He put on his gloves and his boots.

He put a little coat on Top.

He and Top went out into the soft snow.

The other children saw Timothy and Top.

They all came running.

Their dogs came running too.

"What's his name?" asked the children.

"Top," said Timothy.

"Does he bite?" asked one boy.

"Yes," said Timothy, "he bites."

"Does he bark?" asked another.

Timothy Trotter said nothing.

He went into his house.

Top went with him.

The other children went with him.

Their dogs stayed outside.

"When will Top bark?" Timothy asked.

"When he is older," said Mrs. Trotter.

"He's just a puppy," said Mr. Trotter.

"A new baby does not talk.

A new puppy does not bark."

"Don't some puppies bark?" asked Timothy.

"Mine did.

And he was little, too," said one boy.

"So did mine," said a girl.

"And so did ours," said the other children.

Timothy Trotter's mother looked
at Timothy Trotter's father.
"Give Top a good dinner now.
Perhaps he will bark tomorrow."

In the morning the milkman came.

Top did not bark.

The milkman said, "He's a nice dog.

Too bad he cannot bark."

Timothy said, "He's too new to bark."

The postman came.

Top did not bark.

The postman said, "He cannot say bow-wow.

Maybe he will say meow."

"He's a puppy, not a kitten," said Timothy.

A neighbor came to borrow sugar.

Top did not bark.

The neighbor said, "He's been here a week.

Will he ever bark?"

Timothy said, "I think he will—tomorrow."

Tomorrow came.

Top did not bark.

Timothy Trotter looked at Top.

Top looked at Timothy Trotter.

Timothy did not say a word.

Top did not give a bark.

And—because it was dog-walking time—

Timothy put on his hat and his jacket.

He put on his gloves and his boots.

He put a little coat on Top.

He and Top went out into the soft snow.

The children came running.

Their dogs came running.

Timothy did not say a word.

Top did not give a bark.

Timothy and Top walked through the soft snow.

The other children followed.

Their dogs followed.

They all turned the corner.

They all passed many people.

They all passed many houses.

19

Soon they came to a pet shop.

It was Mr. Catterwaller's pet shop.

Timothy and Top went inside.

The other children went inside.

Their dogs went inside.

Mr. Catterwaller was talking to his parrot.

He stopped talking to his parrot.

Mrs. Catterwaller was selling bird seed.

She stopped selling bird seed.

"Look at the kids!

Look at the dogs!" said the parrot.

"What will you have, little people?"

said Mr. Catterwaller.

"My dog does not bark," said Timothy.

"Give him liver," said Mrs. Catterwaller.

"Give him vitamins," said a man.

"Give him horsemeat," said another.

"Give him time!" said Mr. Catterwaller.

"*Awrk!*" said the parrot. "*Give him time!*"

"It's lunch time," said Timothy to Top.

"You can eat even though you cannot bark."

They started for home.

The other children followed.

The dogs followed.

They all passed people.

They all passed the same houses.

They all turned the same corner.

And—

There it happened!

Suddenly Top stood still.

Timothy fell.

Suddenly two big brown dogs stood still.

The boy with them fell.

The big brown dogs had long ears.

Socks covered their ears.

The socks kept their long ears out of the snow.

But Top had never seen socks on a dog's ears!

Top sat down.

He wagged his tail.

He stood up.

He growled.

And then—

Top BARKED!

He barked and barked!

All the other dogs barked.

The big brown dogs turned and ran.

The boy ran after his big brown dogs.

The children shouted, "Hooray for Top!"

Timothy smiled a big, bright smile.

He wiped the soft snow from his jacket.

Then Timothy Trotter and Top went smiling
and barking all the way home.

THE NO-BARK DOG

Reading Level: Level Two. *The No-Bark Dog* has a total vocabulary of 179 words. It has been tested in second grade classes, where it was read with ease.

Uses of this Book: Reading for fun; care of pets. The story proves in a whimsical way that patience reaps its rewards. Timothy's dog Top does not bark. The pet shop man says, "Give him time!" Top himself finally finds the right time.

Word List

All of the 179 words used in *The No-Bark Dog* are listed. Regular possessives and contractions (-'s, -n't, -'ll, -'m) and regular verb forms (-s, -ed, -ing) of words already on the list are not listed separately, but the endings are given in parentheses after the word.

7 Timothy	time	into	what ('s)
Trotter ('s)	put	the	asked
had	on	soft	said
a	hat	snow	does
new	and	**8** other	bite (s)
dog (s) ('s)	jacket	children	one
his	he ('s)	saw	boy
name	gloves	they	yes
was	boots	all	bark (ing) (ed)
Top	little	came	another
now	coat	running	**9** nothing
it ('s)	went	their	house (s)
walking	out	too	with

him
stayed
outside
10 when
will
is
older
Mrs.
just
puppy
Mr.
baby
not
talk (ing)
11 don't
some
puppies
mine
did
girl
so
ours
12 mother
looked
at
father
give
good
dinner
now
perhaps
tomorrow

13 in
morning
milkman
nice
to
postman
cannot
say
bow-wow
maybe
meow
kitten
15 neighbor
borrow
sugar
been
here
week
ever
think
16 word
17 because
19 walked
through
followed
turned
corner
passed
many
people
houses
20 soon

pet
shop
Catterwaller's
inside
21 parrot
stopped
selling
bird
seed
22 look
kids
have
little
23 liver
vitamins
man
horsemeat
time
awrk
24 lunch
eat
even
though
started
for
home
25 same
there
happened
26 suddenly
stood
still

fell
them
big
brown
had
long
ears
socks
covered
kept
of
but
never
seen
on

27 sat
down
wagged
tail
up
growled

28 ran
after
shouted
hooray

29 smile (ing) (d)
bright
wiped
from
way
home

The Follett BEGINNING-TO-READ Books

Purpose of the Beginning-to-Read Books: To provide easy-to-read materials that will appeal to the interests of primary children. Careful attention is given to vocabulary load and sentence length, but the first criterion is interest to children.

Reading Levels: These books are written at three reading levels, indicated by one, two, or three dots beneath the *Beginning-to-Read* symbol on the back cover. *Level One* books can be read by first grade children in the last half of the school year. As children increase their reading ability they will be able to enjoy *Level Two* books. And as they grow further in their reading ability they will progress to *Level Three* books. Some first grade children will read *Level Two* and *Level Three* books. Many third graders, and even some fourth graders, will read and enjoy *Level One* and *Level Two* books, as well as *Level Three* books. The range of interest of *Beginning-to-Read* books stretches far beyond their reading level.

Use of the Beginning-to-Read Books: Because of their high interest and readability, these books are ideal for independent reading by primary children—at school, in the library, and at home. The books may also be incorporated into the basic reading program to develop children's interests, expand their vocabularies, and improve word-attack skills. It has been suggested that they might serve as the foundation for a skillfully directed reading program. Many *Beginning-to-Read* books correlate with the social studies, science, and other subject fields. All will help children grow in the language arts. Children will read the *Beginning-to-Read* books with confidence, with success, and with real enjoyment.

LONGFELLOW SCHOOL
4500 Calhoun Street
Gary, Indiana 46408

W SCHOOL
Calhoun Street
Gary, Indiana 46408

98